EAGLET AND THE RIVER

Written and Illustrated by Wendy Leptien Moore

Order this book online at www.trafford.com
or email orders@trafford.com

Most Trafford titles are also available at major online book retailers.

Printed in the United States of America.

ISBN: 978-1-4269-5477-1 (sc)
ISBN: 978-1-4269-5478-8 (hc)

Library of Congress Control Number: 2011900110

Trafford rev. 02/09/2011

 www.trafford.com

North America & international
toll-free: 1 888 232 4444 (USA & Canada)
phone: 250 383 6864 ♦ fax: 812 355 4082

Dedication

To Mom and Dad

To my sons, Jason and Jeffrey, and my husband, Jim

To my nieces and nephews

To the elementary school children who have

shared my classroom

1976 - 2011

Table of Contents

Chapter I – The Storm

A flash of lightning lit up the sky. Two baby eagles huddled in their nest in the branches of a tall pine. Eaglet, the smallest of the two, buried his head under his wings… wings that enabled him to move about the nest, hop to nearby limbs…wings too young to fly.

Thunder clapped overhead. Eaglet peeked out of the nest and listened for his parents' call. He had been practicing for his first flight. How he wished to soar and dive through the sky like his parents. He settled back into the nest as dark clouds moved across the sky and droplets of rain began to fall.

Nearby, two gray squirrels, one light and one dark, leaped from branch to branch chattering about the storm. Pausing next to Eaglet one called, "We better head for cover! Looks like rain!"

"It sure does," replied the other. "Big storm headed this way. More rain means more water and the stream can't hold much more. "

"Where does it all go? The rain, the rushing water…?"

"Into the stream, to the river, to the sea…remember the stories?" answered the dark gray squirrel.

Eaglet listened carefully. He had never been far from the nest; and therefore, he knew nothing of the stream on the forest floor. Curiously, he lifted his head above the branches and chirped, "What are you talking about? What stream?"

"The stream below us," the dark squirrel replied. "Down there, little eagle. Don't you know? This stream joins many others to form the river," he explained. "Just above Beaver Pond."

"Heh, I'm getting wet. Let's head for home," called the light gray squirrel. Waving to Eaglet, they turned and disappeared into a large hole in the tree.

Puzzled, Eaglet turned to his sister, "Do you know there is a stream below us? A stream that leads to a river?"

"I sure do. This morning while you were roosting with Mother, Father told me stories about the feeding grounds at the river. Every morning and evening a group of eagles follows the stream below. They soar and circle together – it's called kettling. They chase each other, do barrel rolls, and dive-bomb. When we can fly, we can join them! When we go to the river, we can fish, too! Once we can fly, we can do anything!"

"Speaking of fish, I'm hungry! Will they be back soon?"

"They fish in the morning and then again at dusk. Father said they'll be home when the sun sets in the West, beyond our forest, beyond the river valley, beyond ... somewhere called the ocean. Don't worry; they'll be home before dark." Glancing at the menacing sky, Eaglet sighed, "It looks pretty dark to me."

Strong winds muscled the tree branches as the two young eaglets crouched deeper into the nest. Dense rain clouds darkened the sky. Lightning flashed and thunder crashed as a curtain of rainfall drenched the forest.

Suddenly, a bolt of lightning struck. Craaack! A section of the tree splintered from the main trunk ripping the nest in two. Branches that had cradled the eagles, now dangled in the air. Other branches and twigs remained attached to the tree. The eaglets, torn apart, frantically called to one another. Hanging over the rushing water Eaglet lifted his wings. If only I could fly, he thought. Crack…Snap…! Both of the eaglets let out shrill calls, gripping the shifting branches as they began to fall. Down Eaglet went! Down with the branches into the stream! A sharp pain shot through his shoulder. He closed his eyes, letting go of the nesting twigs, his only tie to home. Above, the other eaglet clung to the shredded remains of the nest, the eagle aeries, the eaglets' home.

Then, a darting shadow dove into the swirling waters. A small bird, a water ouzel, grabbed Eaglet's leg and pulled him out of the rapids towards the shore. Eaglet raised his head to thank the ouzel who nodded quietly and flew off into the night.

The waters of the eddy lapped against the shore where Eaglet lay. Exhausted and shaken, he pulled himself out of the muddy pool and onto the grassy bank. The rain beat lightly on his back as the sounds of lightning and thunder faded in the distance. He laid his head to one side and drifted off to sleep - the ouzel but a faint memory.

Chapter II – The Headwaters

Early the next morning, the same two squirrels sat at Eaglet's side whispering to one another.

"Should we wake him up?"

"No, let him rest."

"But, it's dawn. Time to wake up!"

"Just wait…Look…He's opening his eyes."

Eaglet lifted his head and asked, "Where am I?"

"You're at the headwaters of the river," said one of the squirrels. "We saw you fall. The waters carried you downstream and a small bird pulled you from the torrent."

"I remember the bird, small and strong." Eaglet dropped his head and sighed, "I must be so far from my nest. My shoulder aches. My wing…I think it's broken. I'll never fly." Tearfully, he whispered, "I'll never find my way home."

Running to his side, the first squirrel said, "Now just a minute, little fellow. You're not far from home." The other squirrel exclaimed, "And never, say never! Your wing will heal. You will fly. You will fly home!"

Wondering, Eaglet tilted his head, "How do you know?"

A soft smile stretched from ear to ear and the squirrel answered, "Those of us who live along the river understand our place, and you shall too. Trust yourself and listen to the voice within you. It will guide you downstream. There is a right time and a right place for everyone in the river life mosaic. Someday the pieces will fit. Get back on the river, face the changing currents, and let the river carry you home. Believe in yourself and you will fly home."

Eaglet puffed up his chest. He felt hopeful. He felt important. He felt change.

"Here," said one squirrel. "Take this branch. Let the waters carry you to Beaver Pond. Talk to the beavers. They'll know how to help you."

Eaglet clung to the branch that the squirrels had dragged into the water. They pushed him into the current and called, "Hang on! You'll be there by nightfall!"

"Are you sure this is the way? How will I know?"

"Just follow the river," they called as they scampered away.

Chapter III – Beaver Pond

For most of the day, Eaglet braved the rushing river. He rode the wild rapids that swept him downstream. Through rushing waters, past boulders and around bends, Eaglet endured. The helpless fledgling held tightly to the branch that bobbed, swirled, and twisted out of control in the current. Hoping to find calm water, Eaglet hunted for a way to get to the shore.

"Hmm," he thought. "There's no turning back." Remembering the squirrels' words, he knew he must follow the river. How he wished to get off this rollercoaster ride.

Two large boulders loomed ahead. Eaglet clung tightly to the branch as the torrent swung him around into a deep hole on the far side of the rocks. The water pulled him under, then set him free. Drenched, he crawled atop the branch one more time and shook the water from his head. Defeated, Eaglet sighed, "I don't think I can handle one more set of rapids." His wing hung at his side.

But the river changed. Much to his surprise, the river now ran deep and wide. The surface glistened with ripples and spirals and Eaglet's thoughts drifted home:

Prepare, practice, persevere…

I remember Father's words: "You must have perseverance."

Perseverance…What was that? Something about obstacles? Something about going on. So I must go on. Keep hopping. Keep gaining strength. I must return to my nest, my world, my home.

Eaglet murmured, "I have to stay on the river now...I must go on. Persevere". He drifted into deeper water, deeper yet calm.

The river flowed through a meadow carrying the weary traveler into Beaver Pond. He felt the late afternoon sun on his back. "You'll be there by dusk," he remembered the squirrels saying. In the shallows, he let go of the branch, reached the shore and collapsed on the bank. Eaglet wondered about his family. Are they searching for me? Will I see them again? I must return home. I must believe in me. Maybe the beavers can help. But how?

At dusk, four beavers, a mother and her three kits, surfaced and climbed onto the shore. The large female gnawed on a birch tree on the bank. The trunk tipped and fell to the ground. She dragged it to the water.

Hidden in the brush, a bobcat crept toward the beaver kits who were chewing on small branches at the pond's edge. Sensing danger, Eaglet knew he must warn the young beavers. A shrill call pierced the air. The mother beaver lifted her head and spotted the bobcat approaching her young.

The large cat crept closer. As he was about to pounce, the mother beaver plunged into the pond, and slapped the water with her tail! Slap! Slap! Slap!

Alarmed, the kits dashed for the pond as the bobcat leapt towards them. The angry mother appeared and gnashed her teeth into the cat's left haunch. Wincing in pain, he rolled to the ground. Then, he rose and turned with bared teeth and outstretched claws. The mother scrambled to the shore and dove to safety. The pond water stilled. Defeated, the bobcat paused at the water's edge to lick his wound. He limped into the woods and disappeared in the brush.

Eaglet's heart pounded just as it had in the raging waters of the stream.

"Boy, that was a close one," he gasped. "Those young beavers were so vulnerable. Glad I was here to warn them. They must have been frightened. Just like me on the river. Just different. I guess everyone meets danger and fear in their own way. I'm glad I'm here. I don't feel so alone and vulnerable now. I just helped them...maybe now they can help me."

His throat was dry, so he dragged his wing to the shore. He quenched his thirst at a trickle of water that fed the pond. Nightfall had come and a crescent moon cast a soft light on the pond's surface. He glanced towards the lodge where the beavers had sought refuge. Now, the still waters of Beaver Pond provided a safe place for him. In the quiet of the night, his thoughts drifted home. A soft whisper comforted him:

"Someday you will join us in the skies. You must prepare for flight. One day soon, you will fly and soar to greatness."

"I don't feel so great right now," he thought.

Later, in the moonlit evening, the beavers paddled through the glassy waters towards Eaglet. They purred as they slid onto the bank. Rubbing their faces and whimpering, they turned to Eaglet.

"Thanks for the warning. Thought that old bobcat left days ago," said the mother beaver.

"Oh, you're welcome," said Eaglet. "That was a close one!"

"So what can we do for you, little eaglet?"

"The squirrels sent me here. They told me to come to Beaver Pond."

"This is the place. We'll return at sunrise. Then we'll see what we can do for you." Quietly, they slipped back into the pond. "A small beginning," Eaglet thought, "But a beginning…someone to talk to, someone to help me return home."

Chapter IV – The Builders

At dawn a lone beaver's wake rippled the surface. The beaver grunted as she climbed onto the bank. "Good morning, little eagle. Now, what brings you to Beaver Pond?"

Eaglet stared at her huge webbed feet and large, flat scaly tail. He told the beaver about the storm and how the lightning had struck the tree; how he had fallen into the stream, met the squirrels and traveled to Beaver Pond. Eaglet gazed at the beaver searching for some answers in her eyes. "Where do I go from here? How do I get home?" he asked anxiously.

The beaver chuckled. "At Beaver Pond we believe a beaver's work is never done until it's done. You just have to stick with it. That's right, Sonny. You just have to stick with it."

"Stick with it? Stick with what?" Eaglet asked.

"Stick with anything you try to do. Stick with your plan. Get back on the river. At Boulder Bend, look for the stone face on the canyon wall. Below is the cave of the Canyon Bear. That bear knows everything! He will tell you where to meet the salmon. They know where to find the whales, the wisest creatures of all. The whales will have an answer for you. You must follow the river to the sea."

She added, "First, we will splint your wing so that it will heal. Then we'll build you a sturdy raft that will carry you down the river."

"But how will I get beyond your dam?" asked Eaglet. The tangled mass of branches, twigs, and mud seemed impossible to pass.

"We'll fix that!" replied the beaver. "Much work to do. Must get started," she added as she dove into the water. "We'll be back soon!"

As promised, the beavers returned in the early afternoon. They attached a splint to Eaglet's wing and placed him on a log raft. Eaglet found the finely woven rope they had attached to the front of the raft. The beavers pulled the river traveler through a series of canals and back into the water beyond the dam.

"This is great. My own raft!" Eaglet called as the currents pulled him down river. "Thanks again." His shoulder was stiff. The splint was heavy. But he was happy to be on the river again. His journey began to take on new meaning. Eaglet listened to a voice within whispering, "Follow the river home."

Chapter V – Narrow Escape

The river was deeper and moving quickly. Strong currents tugged at the raft as Eaglet steered towards the right bank avoiding the huge boulders in the river. He felt the warm sun on his back as he bounced through a set of rapids.

Suddenly, the raft jerked and stopped. Eaglet clung to the edge of the raft as rushing water poured over him. His sore wing lay in the swift current and his heart pounded. The tow rope was caught on a forked branch that stuck out of the water. His only hope was to tear at the rope to break the snag's monstrous grip.

Two small field mice scampered on the bank. Jumping from stone to stone, then boulder to boulder, they ran towards Eaglet.

"Look! He's caught! He's going to drown!" shouted one mouse. "We have to help him."

"Oh no! Not me! He's an eagle, a raptor...he's dangerous!" squeaked the other.

"Oh, come on. We can just gnaw through the rope to free him and then head back to shore...hurry!"

The young mice leaped onto the bow and chewed through the rope. Suddenly, the raft broke free of the snag and spun around in the swirling waters. Eaglet blinked his eyes and turned to thank the mice who cowered in fear at the far corner of the raft.

Chapter VI – Newfound Friends

"Don't be afraid," whispered Eaglet. "I was in real trouble and you saved me. I wish you no harm."

"But, we fear all birds of prey and tremble in the shadows of your great wings."

"Great wings? Just look at me. I can't even fly. Today we meet as friends," said Eaglet.

The mice perched on their hind legs and nervously tossed their heads from side to side looking for the shore. "I hear the waterfall! The falls are coming. We must get ashore! We must get off the river now!"

The two small mice leaped into the water and swam through the current with Eaglet's tow rope clenched in their mouths. As soon as they tied the raft to a branch on the shore, a chorus of fidgeting mice called from the bank. "Squeak, squeak, squeak!" Eaglet looked curiously at a weed basket they help upon their backs.

"We'll carry you! Come on! We'll take you down the Misty Falls stairway. We can do it! Climb on!"

"Where's the Misty Falls stairway?" asked Eaglet.

"Beyond those trees," squeaked the smallest mouse.

"Just around the corner," said his brother.

"It's the only way to return to the river – you must come with us," called another.

Eaglet knew he had to go with the mice. Yet he didn't want to leave his raft.

"Don't worry," said one of the mice. "We'll push the raft into the water and let it go over the falls. We'll find it below. We'll save it. But we must hurry!"

Eaglet nodded his head and hopped into the basket balanced on the backs of the mice. Over green, mossy steps, the newfound friends carried Eaglet down a forty foot stairway. They placed him at the base of the falls where the churning waters had tossed the raft like a leaf onto the shore.

"How can I ever thank you?" asked Eaglet.

"Ah, it's nothing…just watch where you're going and keep an eye out for the bobcat," the last mouse called as they ran away.

Eaglet pushed himself away from the shore through the mist. As he drifted into the main current, he strained his neck to gaze at the top of the falls. His head jerking from side to side, he searched for movement. He was aware of his keen eyesight and searched for the mice. Yet, all that could be seen or heard was the rushing and falling of water over Misty Falls.

Evening shadows began to fall. After a few more bends in the river, Eaglet tediously tied the raft to a large root on the shore using his beak and one strong talon. Another day on the river was over. Tomorrow he would begin his search for the bear.

Chapter VII – The River Otters

Colors spread across the early morning sky. Eaglet was thirsty and drank some river water. He was very hungry. His plan for the day became clear; he had to find food.

The river snaked its way through a wide canyon. Large boulders lined the shore and tangled tree roots exposed from rushing waters, stretched along the bank. Small, sandy beaches also dotted parts of the river. As Eaglet floated downstream, something caught his eye.

Splash! Splash! Splash! He felt the spray of water upon his back as three playful river otters dove beneath his raft. A fourth otter, a large female, peered out from her den in a gnarled root base. The young eagle steered his raft toward the beach. The otters continued their chase game, as Eaglet watched them jump, dive and roll through the water. He eagerly awaited their sudden surfacing and puppy-like squeals.

Three otters hopped onto the shore, perched on their front flippers, and tipped their heads towards Eaglet. Their beady eyes curiously searched the raft, and the wet, feathered newcomer to their beach.

Laughing at the funny otters, Eaglet flapped his wings and greeted them. "Hello, I'm Eaglet. I'm trying to find my way home."

The smallest otter rolled over and flopped into his sister; she rolled over twice and plowed into her brother; he rolled three times and bumped into his mother who had joined them; she rolled over four times and jumped onto the nearest boulder. "Ready for a swim?" she asked.

"No, I don't swim," Eaglet said. ""But I can fly... uh, er, I mean, I almost know how to fly. My wing was injured when I fell from my nest in a storm and I've been trying to get home ever since."

"We're swimmers—not much we can do for you if you can't swim," the otter replied. She dove into the water followed by the others.

"But wait! Wait!" shouted Eaglet. "There must be something you can do to help me. Maybe I can swim. If it'll help me get home, I'll try anything."

Silence. Disappointed and alone, Eaglet stared at the rippling waters. His hopes of ever getting home seemed dashed upon the rocks.

Then, one by one, the otters returned, each one holding a small fish in his mouth.

"Breakfast, coming up," called one.

"We thought you might be hungry," chimed another.

"One fish, two fish, three fish, four! Eat these up and we'll fish for more!" Eaglet's eyes opened wide as the fish flew through the air and landed at his side. Then he gulped down his meal and rested in the sand.

"So… How about it?"

"How about what?" Eaglet asked.

"How about a swim?"

"But, I can't swim," said Eaglet.

"Have you ever tried?" asked one of the otters.

"Well, no…"

"You never know 'til you try," called the three.

Eaglet laughed, "Sure. Why not?"

The otters climbed onto the beach, lifted his legs and wings and dropped him into the river. Skimming the surface of the pool, they carried him through the water.

Moving his feet, fluttering, then flapping his wings, Eaglet began to swim. A strange feeling came over him. How he had feared the water. Now the calm water, the furried friends, and the energy pulsing through his wings as he exercised them all came together and gave him new hope. This was unfamiliar territory, the unknown; yet he felt he now could do anything. Perhaps he could soon fly...The otters cheered him on and swam at his side as he paddled his feet through the water and back to shore with confidence.

"The fish were delicious. I liked the swim. I'd stay and play but I need to find the Cave Bear. Am I close to Boulder Bend?"

The otters nodded to one another and one said, "After the next bend in the river, look for the stone face. You can't miss it! The bear's den is just below." He signaled to the others, "Next stop, Boulder Bend!"

Well-fed and self-assured, Eaglet launched his raft. The otters appeared at each corner and guided him downriver.

The morning sun dried his feathers and his injured wing felt stronger after food and exercise.

"This is as far as we go," the lead otter called. "Boulder Bend is right around the next corner. You're on your own now."

"Right around the corner? Are you sure?" There was no answer. Eaglet looked downstream, flapped his wings, and hopped about the raft anxiously awaiting his meeting with the bear.

Chapter VIII – On to Boulder Bend

Steep canyon walls rose on each side of the river. The rock cliffs, draped in moss and sketched with time gone by, jutted out into the blue sky. Huge granite boulders, sanded by rushing waters, loomed on each side of Eaglet.

An island of brush, broken tree limbs, and debris divided the river. Drifting to the left, into a slow-moving pool, Eaglet tied up to a willow branch along the bank. He rested on a clump of grass and listened for the distant call of eagles as twilight brought a symphony of sounds to his ear.

It was at twilight that his parents would return from their final flight of the day. It was twilight that reminded him of home, the warmth and comfort of his treetop nest. It was twilight that now told him it was time to rest.

In the light of the half moon, the bobcat from Beaver Pond crouched in the brush at the river's edge. "Easy catch tonight…an injured bird," he snickered. Tail flicking back and forth, he crept through the bushes towards his prey! Then he pounced. He had Eaglet clutched in his claws.

"The bobcat!" squeaked a tiny voice.

"He's got Eaglet!" cried another. Perched atop a large boulder on the bank, the woodland mice formed a circle. Secretly, they had followed Eaglet downstream for they had feared he would be hunted by the hungry cat.

They lifted their tiny fists together and shouted, "Charge!"

Eaglet's heart pounded. The bobcat did not flinch. The mice scrambled off the boulder, down the bank and into the brush. Timing their target, the mice attacked. Half of them chomped on his tail while the other half yanked on his whiskers. The bobcat howled, released his grip on Eaglet and dashed away. Stunned, Eaglet lay in the dust.

"Hooray! Hooray!" cheered the mice.

"Are you alright?" the smallest mouse asked.

Eaglet smiled. "Yes, I'm alright. At the pond I warned the beavers about the bobcat; now you've saved me from his clutches. Where did you come from, anyway? I thought I was alone."

"Oh, we followed you from Misty Falls. Just wanted to make sure you were alright."

"Yeh, I'm O.K. - just a little tired." Exhausted, he lay his head down and fell asleep. The mice curled up at his side through the night. At sunrise, they headed home to the forest floor.

Chapter IX – The Bear

Early the next morning, Eaglet opened his eyes and spotted a reflection in the water. He stared at what appeared to be a mouth, a nose, and two large eyes. Slowly, he turned his head toward the steep canyon wall. A weathered crack in the rocks seemed to smile. A ridge, covered with clumps of moss, wrinkled like a nose. Two boulders, painted with black lichens, twinkled. "This is it! The stone face!" he thought. Curious but unsure, he paused. Then he hopped to the entrance of the dark cave beneath the rocky ledge.

A large black bear lumbered out of the cave.

"You're new around here," he yawned. "Or is it me? I've been asleep for months. Just heard the birds of Spring this morning. What brings you to Boulder Bend?"

"The beavers sent me to see you. I am following the river home, but it feels like I'm going the wrong way." He hopped up and down and flapped his wings as he told the bear all about his journey so far. "So…can you help me? Where do I go now?"

The bear brushed a bee away from his ear and plopped down next to Eaglet.

"Boulder Bend is my home – great fishing spot. Spring! I wait here for the salmon run. Just look over there. That bear has already caught his fish for the day."

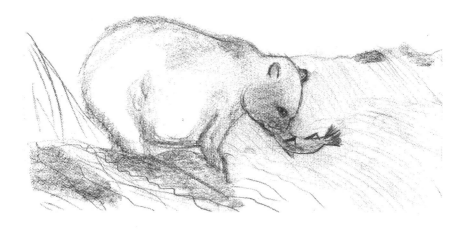

Nodding his head, the bear continued. "Looks like the salmon are returning. Within a few days salmon will fill these waters to spawn. They have traveled far. The life cycle of the salmon begins and ends right here. They're just part of the picture, part of river life. I guess you could say I'm the caretaker of this neck of the woods."

Listening carefully to the bear, Eaglet tilted his head and asked, "What do I have to do with the salmon? Tell me more."

The bear stretched and began to slowly pace in front of the cave. "You need to talk to the salmon. They tell stories of the Wide River Valley, Seal Rock and the Great Gray Whale. They know of the sea."

"Is that it? Is that all you have to say?"

The bear smiled. "Yep, that's it. Talk to the salmon. Follow the river, little eaglet. It will carry you home."

"Then I must be going." Eaglet hopped onto the raft and centered himself. Raising his injured wing for the first time, he bid farewell to the bear. With a wink of his eye, the bear gently nodded and headed back into his cave.

Chapter X – The Salmon

Eaglet glanced back at the cave and then set forth upon the river.

Short hops and wing flapping carried him from one end of the raft to the other.

The river had changed course and broadened. Grasses, brush, and willows lined the bank. Eaglet studied the birds fluttering in the trees. He studied their wings, he heard their calls. "Someday," he thought, "my wings will carry me home. But for now, I'll let the river carry me to the sea."

Silver streaks downstream caught his eye. The surface of the water rippled with the salmons' splashing tails.

"Hello, hello!" Eaglet called to the salmon as they flipped and flopped over the rocky shallows of the river.

"Hello! The bear sent me to see you. He told me that you would help me find my way to the sea." Eaglet told his story and added, "If I make it to the sea, then I can go home. I'm not sure how or why, but the animals have told me it is so."

The silvery head of the first salmon rose out of the water. She spoke softly, "We are going home to spawn in the waters of Boulder Bend. It is who we are and what we do." Eaglet noticed the bumps, bruises, and tears, the scars of her long journey. His bumps and bruises ached too.

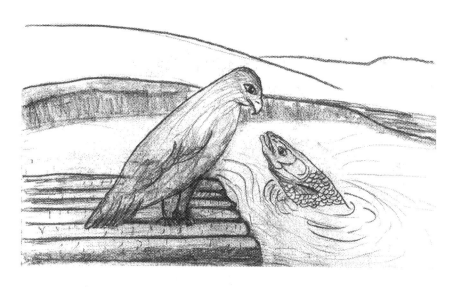

She continued, "I was born here. I will lay my eggs here. Then I will die." The rippling water muffled the salmon's soft, tired voice. Eaglet leaned closer. "Some of our kind are raised in a hatchery and released into the river. They, too, know where to begin and end their journey to and from the sea. I was born at Boulder Bend and there I shall return. My bumps and bruises, scrapes and cuts...many are from my trip up the fish ladder. Some of us get channeled into the hatchery and some of us continue upstream to our natural spawning grounds. I am weak and tired after climbing the ladder. Now, I'm almost home."

"I think I'm almost home too," whispered Eaglet. "Tell me now…which way is my home?"

"Follow the river," the salmon replied. "Once the river meets the sea, find the seals who will escort you to the Gray Whales. Your timing must be right for the whale migrations only pass the mouth of the river at certain times of the year. Some salmon runs are in the Spring and many are in the Fall. Meet the seals at Seal Rock on the next full moon. Then, seek the Great Gray Whale and discover your way home.

Eaglet was disappointed. He thought the salmon would have the answer. He said, "You mean, stay on the river and go all the way to the ocean? Meet the seals at Seal Rock on the next full moon?" he repeated. The salmon slipped into the water. He searched the sky for a glimpse of the evening moonrise.

Eaglet drifted towards the bank. He tied the rope around a boulder on the shore feeling a soft breeze on his back. He thought, "There is a driving force behind the life cycles of all of my river friends. The same force is within me. I feel it now. I will learn to fly and find my way home. I feel the winds that steer me now."

With this new understanding, Eaglet rested on the shore in the light of the waxing moon while the salmon swam past him on their way to Boulder Bend.

Chapter XI – The Warren

Sunrise. Eaglet stretched his talons and preened his feathers in the sunlight. Exercising his wings, a newfound strength pulsed from within...I will fly. I can feel it now.

A warbler's morning song filled the air as Eaglet's raft drifted over the shimmering water. He surveyed the surrounding foothills through stands of alder that lined the banks. A hummingbird flitted into the trees above him. The swiftness reminded him of the small ouzel that had pulled him to shore so many days ago.

On the hillside he noticed the grass moving; an opening…, then dirt, rocks and dust. A rabbit appeared. Eaglet fixed his gaze on the spot. Rabbits! And more rabbits! This must be Rabbit Run…this is the rabbit warren that Mother described:

Rabbit Run is where you can practice. You will ride the thermal updrafts. Flying…flying with wings flat and motionless…flying in spirals above the warming hills. Watch for the hummingbirds. Study their flight – swift, brief, beautiful. Also, look for the Monarch butterfly. This is a resting place for the yearly Monarch migration, another life cycle. Just amazing. Rabbit Run is a place that all must see!

Eaglet steered to shore and caught a glimpse of a hawk swooping down into the tall grass. He scrambled up the bank and began taking two and three foot flights above the wild orange poppies. Pausing, he watched a covey of quail scurry across his path.

Then, he glanced to the top of the knoll.

Two cottontails peered out from behind the brush. Curious about the erratic flight of the young eagle, they hopped down the mound.

"Now, Cotton! We're awfully far from the warren," one rabbit cautioned.

"I know. I know," Cotton answered. "I'll be just a minute. I have to take a closer look at this bird. I'm next in line for warren scout! Besides, what's that eaglet doing on the ground, anyway?"

In the thicket, a twig snapped. The rabbits froze. Cotton signaled, "The bushes...quiet!" Crouched in the brush, a female red fox held a predatory stance.

Then, the silence was broken by a piercing cry, sharp barks and yips. The fox turned towards her den stunned to see a hawk carrying off one of her young. The remaining kits huddled in a hollow log. The hawk lit in an open-limbed tree and the limp, tiny legs dangled in the air.

Eaglet observed. He wanted to tell the hawk to let the kit go. If the hawk let the kit go, the red fox would retreat. If the red fox retreated, the rabbits would return to the safety of their warren. Predator and prey. Where did he fit? He wanted to help.

Yet, he stood still. The stillness spoke to him. "Trust. The river is calling me. Move forward and trust. Continue your journey." He scrambled down the bank and got back on the river.

He glanced back at the grassy hill. The hawk had dropped its prey. The rabbits had disappeared into a burrow. The fox, grabbing her kit by the neck, headed back to her den. The hummingbird darted to a higher limb. Eaglet looked for the butterfly.

He knew they would be arriving soon but he had to go.

Chapter XII – The Wide River Valley

The river snaked its way through the wide valley blanketed in fog where brilliant sprigs of green grass colored the water's edge. The gray brush budded under a canopy of trees. The deep muddy waters lapped against the banks of the wide river where statuesque Snowy Egrets fed along the shore. More change.

Snow geese, in formation, flew overhead. Eaglet listened to their distant calls in the fog. He called back to them through the misty blanket covering the Pacific Flyway, the winter home of the geese. His parents had told him of the migratory ways of the snow geese – their instinctual, "voice inside" migration North and South every year.

Eaglet called again…but the air was still. "Hmm…," he thought. "Noone is there. But someone is here…that's me…maybe something inside of me can lead me home."

Tall grasses lined the river. The raft drifted into a large marsh. Eaglet remembered that only a short time ago, the squirrels had pulled his vessel into the strong current and bid him farewell.

Now, wood ducks nested in the damp weeds close to

the Great Blue Heron standing at the water's edge.

A loud rush of air

Flapping wings...

Snow geese rose from the still waters and

Took flight...

The geese soared above Eaglet, circled three times and

landed with orchestrated motion in the neighboring

pond.

Suddenly, a small wood duck appeared and quacked,

"You're new here?"

"Yes, I am…I'm following the river to the ocean. Am I close to the river's end?"

"Just three more bends in the river. You'll see the dunes. Maybe a day's journey away."

"Well, I just saw the geese and I wondered what they are doing here."

"Oh, they come at different times during the year. This is their resting place in the Pacific Flyway. Soon, they'll be heading north, home."

"Home?" queried Eaglet. "They are going home… maybe they can help me."

Summoning his three brothers, the wood duck tugged on the frazzled tow rope and pulled Eaglet's raft through the tufts of sawgrass. A large white Snow Goose approached Eaglet.

"So far from home?"

Eaglet nodded and then told the goose his river story.

"What you need now is the wind in your sails," cackled the goose.

"Wind in my sails?" questioned Eaglet. "I have no sails and I feel no wind today."

"We shall fix that! My sisters and brothers shall each give you a single feather. Then the river rats will make a feathered sail for your raft. The afternoon winds will come and carry you the final distance to the sea. Gather the feathers. Take them to the crafty rats. This evening, you shall have a fine, feathered sail for your raft and the delta winds shall carry you to the sea."

Eaglet thanked the snow goose. What an idea…the wind, the water, the way. The wood ducks pulled the raft to a sandy bank where the rats greeted the tired traveler. They all discussed the project.

By nightfall, a white billowy sail fluttered above the raft. A gibbous moon cast a shimmering light across the delta, Eaglet's last haven before his sojourn to the sea.

Chapter XIII – Delta and Beyond

The river had widened. The surrounding hills were dotted with sparse vegetation. The wind-swept dunes lay ahead and seagulls glided on the airy wind currents. A cool, dense fog blanketed the dunes and channeled its way up the mouth of the river. The damp salty air chilled Eaglet; yet, he felt the warmth of anticipation inside. Only a short time ago, the wood ducks had pulled Eaglet's vessel onto the river.

How the river had changed. How he had changed. His wing had healed. His new friendships had guided him. His own courage and tenacity had carried him the course of the river. The river had been his quide and provider, the creator of his challenges and the insurer of his success. The river, ever-changing, was an ominous caregiver of its inhabitants, their life cycles and their ways. The river had been his friend. He felt ready to face his final quest—the ocean, the Great Gray Whale and his return home.

Hours passed. The raft lodged itself into a thick, sandy shelf on the edge a sandbar centered in the shallows. Eaglet could now see the pounding surf. Stuck again, he thought, "How will I ever get off of this sandbar? How will I ever get beyond the waves? How will I ever get to Seal Rock? To be so close, yet feel so far…"

Just then a seagull lit on his bow of his raft.

"Well…hi there, Bud! What's with the raft? Let's catch a draft and ride the wind!"

Eaglet paused and then answered, "Well…hi there to you too! Wish I could but my wing…oh, never mind… I'm trying to get to Seal Rock. Am I close? That surf looks rough." He dropped his head and sighed, "It's just impossible…I'll never get over the surf wall…I'll never get out to the rock."

"O.K., Bud," the seagull squawked. "Sit tight. I'll be right back."

At the base of the nearby rock ledge, he searched through debris. Returning with a large sack, he proudly spread his collection at Eaglet's feet.

"Let's see," he muttered. "There must be something here." Several gulls alighted nearby and hunted through the pile. Working together, they tied ropes of seaweed to each corner of the raft.

"Heave Ho!" shouted the lead gull. "And up we go!" Eaglet grasped the raft's edge as the gulls transported him through the air. After a sudden drop beyond the rolling surf, Eaglet found himself drifting on the wide, blue sea. Seal Rock was in view. He looked for the gulls…nowhere to be seen. Alone… again…

But know it felt good to be alone. Inside he knew he was just where he was supposed to be. He felt a force from within—a force that spoke of becoming, a force that spoke of home.

Chapter XIV – Seal Rock

Within minutes a company of seals surfaced and surrounded Eaglet. Taking turns, they towed Eaglet toward the colony on Seal Rock. Eaglet eyed an enormous, silky black seal basking in the sun. The fog had lifted and young seals frolicked in the glistening blue waters. The surf splashed over the base of Seal Rock, a weathered sea stack that marked the ocean home of the Great Gray Whale.

"Arf, arf, arf!" Three seal pups dove off the rocks as another spotted seal hauled himself onto a ledge. The escort seals anchored the raft near the head of the colony.Eaglet hopped to a tide pool searching for food, taking a few short flights. He landed in front of the large seal who slowly lifted his head, "So…you've come to ask for help. You must have a good reason for coming all this way."

"I have had a long journey on the river. I'm ready to go home. My wing has healed. I'm ready for my first flight, and I need to find the whales. My river friends told me to come to see you during the full moon. So here I am. They said you would know where to find the whales." Eaglet tilted his head, flapped his wings and waited for a reply.

Shifting his body side to side, the bulky seal reassured the young eagle, "Test your strength and test your wings. Tomorrow, the morning of the full moon, I will take you to the Great Whale."

Chapter XV – Morning of the Full Moon

The full moon touched the horizon as sunrise painted the morning sky. Eaglet's wings caught the cool morning breezes as he fed on rock crabs in the tide pools. He flew short distances from rock to rock feeling pockets of air lifting his wings…flight?

The seals arrived as planned. Eaglet hopped on board and the escort skimmed the glassy water heading out to sea.

Fountain sprays in the distance, marked the whale's location. A fluke appeared just above the surface.

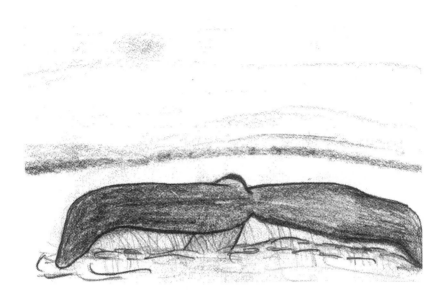

The seals slowed as they approached the herd. Suddenly, an enormous whale breeched, leaping out of the water and falling back into the sea. A young calf swam at her side.

The lead seal barked, "Our timing is right. The whales are heading North from their breeding grounds in the southern seas."

Eaglet's raft and the company of seals rolled with the ocean waves beside the largest of the herd. Her mouth opened slightly, gallons of water filling her baleen. The whale's mouth closed. One large eye opened and locked its gaze on Eaglet.

"Majesty of the skies…Why do you seek me?"

Eaglet began:

I have traveled long and far on the river. The animals sent me to you. I'm ready to fly. I want to soar and dive like an eagle. A real eagle, like my parents. I wish I could fly! I want to fly home.

The whale dove, surfaced and said, "You can fly, little eagle. You must believe in yourself. Listen to your self within…it's the voice, the one, that is always with you. It's just like being home. You are strong and able. Now, you just need to try.…to believe in yourself…and to trust."

"But…the salmon said you would have the answer. I don't get it."

The whale gently smiled and said, "Climb aboard! Together, we have the answer. I will give you a gentle blast from my blowhole to send you on your way. After that, it is your way…your time to fly…the salmon knew that I could give you a lift, or a boost. The rest is up to you."

"We must hurry, though…I will have to catch up with the pod. I am returning to the northern ocean to feed. Within, our force drives us, drives me. Speaks of my home, my way. I understand the force that drives you home. The time is now. Hop on!"

Eaglet took a deep breath, closed his eyes and flapped his wings as hard as he could. The ocean swells gently rocked him as he took pause on the enormous back of the whale. Pulsing blasts of air and water lifted him into the air. He flapped his wings with all his might and chanted, "Fly, Eaglet, fly…you can fly, if you try". He thought he heard a chorus of other voices echo his call.

Then, Eaglet felt the wind. He felt the ocean spray. He felt the warmth of the sun and he took flight. Catching the currents, he glided through the air with ease. This was the moment; this was his time. The animal and ocean guides were all part of this moment with the Great Gray Whale. Now, the strong ocean breezes also lifted his wings. He soared higher and higher in the sky. Flight here, flight over the river, flight home…it was all here and energy surged within the young eagle.

With a final farewell to the whales, seals and seagulls, Eaglet turned toward the river, "This is the river that helped me find my wings, helped me find my way. Now, I'll follow the river home."

Chapter XVI – Home

Eaglet circled above the mouth of the river in the misty air. He understood that the moisture, the immense water droplets of the first storm, the stream, the river and the ocean below were all part of one natural cycle. He had traveled far to find and know where the river has its end. Yes…this is the river's end…and the beginning. Now, he knew…"I am the river," he whispered. "This is my beginning."

His flight took him over the estuary and the rolling hills, home of the fox, the hawk and the rabbits. He continued over the Wide River Valley, home of the Snow Geese, the muskrats, and the ducks. He flew above the river canyon, home of the salmon, the bear, the otters, and the mice. Finally, he soared over the headwaters of the river, home of the beaver and the squirrels. He was flying high and felt like the 'King of the Skies'. He had changed, as does the course of a river, as do the gentle winds.

Eaglet caught a glimpse of a bird, a water ouzel, darting in and out of the rapids in the mountain stream below. Something familiar…

Something beckoned him. He lit on a branch. Familiar smell of pine, treetops, and then…he heard the familiar call of three majestic birds. In the distance he saw the three soaring eagles – Eaglet's family, Eaglet's home.

Epilogue

Down the changing course of a river

Through the stormy winds, the gentle breeze,

The young eagle, now a bird of flight,

Soars above the trees.

As Eaglet soared through the sky, he noticed another

young eagle circling below him.

He wondered if she knew about the river.

He let the winds carry him to her side for he had a story

to tell and

A new day had just begun.

The Headwaters

Beaver Pond

Misty Falls

Boulder Bend

The Warren

Salmon Migration

Wide River Valley

The Delta

Seal Rock

Gray Whale Migration